MOONGOBBLE AND ME
THE EVIL ELVES

MOONGOBBLE AND ME
THE EVIL ELVES

Bruce Coville
ILLUSTRATED BY Katherine Coville

SCHOLASTIC INC.
New York Toronto London Auckland Sydney
Mexico City New Delhi Hong Kong Buenos Aires

ISBN 0-439-79155-3

12 11 10 9 8 7 6 5 4 3 2 1   6 7 8 9 10 /0

Printed in the U.S.A.   40

First Scholastic printing, February 2006

Book design by Lucy Ruth Cummins

The text for this book is set in Historical Fell Type.

The illustrations for this book are rendered in graphite.

For Nathan Dietz

CONTENTS

CHAPTER 1

A CHEESE TOO LONG

Urk the toad sat on one side of the table.

I sat on the other.

Between us was the piece of cheese that used to be our friend, Moongobble the Magician.

Moongobble had turned himself into cheese with a magic spell. That was not unusual—he did it at least once a week. He didn't do it on purpose. It was just that he didn't have very good control of his magic. Most of the time he turned back to himself in a few hours. But he had been cheese since yesterday afternoon, and Urk and I were getting worried.

"Do you think we should send for help?" I asked.

"Who are we going to ask?" snorted Urk. "Fazwad?"

Fazwad is head of the Society of Magicians. He had told Moongobble that unless he performed three Mighty Tasks, he would not be allowed to join.

This worried me. If Moongobble could not join the society, he would not be allowed to do magic anywhere in the kingdom. I liked working for Moongobble—and not just because he paid me a silver penny every day. He was a very good person . . . even if he was not a very good magician.

I glanced at the big yellow chunk on the table. Moongobble certainly couldn't perform his next Mighty Task if he was cheese.

"What will we do if Fazwad shows up before Moongobble turns back?" I asked.

Urk shrugged his bumpy shoulders. "We could pretend Moongobble has gone to visit someone. I don't know if that will fool Fazwad, though. He's pretty good at detecting magic. He's likely to guess this isn't a normal cheese."

At least we had taken Moongobble's hat off the

cheese. That would have been a sure giveaway. Of course, the main reason we moved the hat was to keep the mice who lived inside it from being too tempted. I didn't know what would happen if they nibbled on Moongobble before he turned back—and I didn't want to find out!

I went to the front of the cottage and stepped out. Something hissed above me. Looking up, I saw a little dragon sitting in a nearby tree. He stretched his wings and fluttered down to my shoulder.

This was Fireball. I had met him on our first adventure, and he came back to stay with us. I wanted him to live in our cottage, but Mother does not think dragons and people should live together. Even so, I liked having a dragon for a friend. (You don't

want to think about calling a dragon a "pet"!)

"Is Moongobble still cheese?" asked Fireball.

I nodded.

Below us, at the bottom of the hill, was my village, Pigbone-East-of-the-Mountains. There isn't much to Pigbone, just fifteen cottages. The farthest one belongs to our friend, the Rusty Knight. The closest one is where I live.

I have always lived with Mother. Until a little while ago, my father was missing. But Moongobble and I found him while we were out on the second Mighty Task.

That was the best thing that ever happened to me. It was also one more reason I wanted Moongobble to do well. If he hadn't moved to Pigbone, I still wouldn't have a father.

While I was thinking about this, a little voice asked, "Is this where Moongobble lives?"

I looked around, but couldn't see anyone.

"Down here!" cried the voice.

I looked down, then gasped in surprise.

"Who are *you*?" I cried.

CHAPTER 2

ARFUR'S MISSION

At my feet was a strange-looking contraption. It was about a foot high and had wings that looked as if they came from a giant dragonfly. The wings were mounted above a seat that rested between a pair of wheels about the size of my hands.

Perched in the seat was a man not more than four inches tall. He had pointed ears and a young-looking face.

"My name is Arfur!" he said, shouting up at me. "I need to talk to Moongobble."

"He's inside," I said. Then I added quickly, "But you can't see him now!"

"He'll want to see me," insisted the little man.

I thought about telling him that Moongobble couldn't see anyone until he had eyeballs again. Before I could figure out the best way to say that, Arfur muttered, "Oh, no. Don't tell me he's turned himself into cheese again!"

I nodded, surprised he had figured it out so quickly.

"Let me inside right now," he demanded.

"Better let him in," whispered Fireball, then he fluttered back to his branch.

As I opened the door the little man pumped his feet, pressing them against some pedals. The wings began to flap. A second later the contraption floated into the air.

"It's a winged wonder," muttered Fireball, stretching his own wings and looking at them.

Arfur flew his contraption through the door, circled the room twice, then landed on the table.

"Who are you?" asked Urk. "And what are you doing here?"

"I'll explain later," said Arfur, climbing out of his Winged Wonder. He walked over to the cheese. "I take it this is Moongobble?"

"You take right," croaked Urk.

Arfur opened a pouch that hung at his side and pulled out a handful of shiny dust. He sprinkled the dust over Moongobble. A small explosion made me jump backward. Fireball flapped his wings to keep from falling off his branch.

An instant later Moongobble was sitting in the center of the table, blinking in surprise.

"Arfur!" he cried happily. "How did you get here? Urk! Edward! Meet my friend Arfur. He's one of the elves who helped me when I was a shoemaker!"

Moongobble had told me the day we met that it was helpful elves who first got him interested in magic.

"I'm very pleased to meet you," I said, stepping closer to the table.

"And I you," said Arfur.

"Would you like something to eat?" asked Moongobble.

"A blueberry would be nice," said Arfur.

We all had a snack. As Arfur was licking the last of the blueberry juice from his fingers, Moongobble

said, "What brings you to visit, old friend?"

The little man's face grew serious. "I need your help, Moongobble. My family is in terrible trouble!"

"I will do anything I can!" cried Moongobble. "You know that. What is the problem?"

Arfur's answer was cut off by a buzzing sound.

We heard a loud snap.

Urk groaned.

I couldn't blame him.

Fazwad had arrived.

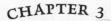

CHAPTER 3

THE THIRD MIGHTY TASK

Fazwad stood just inside the cottage. He had not walked through the door. He had just appeared there.

Sometimes I wondered what would happen if Fazwad tried to appear someplace and something was already in that spot. Like a chair, for example. I thought this would be very interesting to see.

Mother has told me that this is an unworthy thought.

Sneering his usual sneer, Fazwad walked to the table.

I wondered what he would say about Arfur—until

I realized that Arfur was nowhere in sight. Where had he gone?

Fireball, who was clinging to the back of my chair, hissed angrily. Fireball does not like Fazwad.

"Well, well, well—what a nice little gathering," said Fazwad, in a voice that didn't have an ounce of nice in it.

Moongobble and I stood up. Urk just glared.

Fazwad pointed at Moongobble. "I'm here to assign your third Mighty Task." Then he smiled, and added, "Unless you've come to your senses and decided to give up."

"Of course I haven't given up!" said Moongobble.

Fazwad shook his head. "Don't say I didn't give you a chance. All right, here is your next Mighty Task. West of here, in the Forest of Boodle, a band of elves is causing trouble."

Moongobble looked shocked. "But elves are nice!"

"Not all of them," snarled Fazwad. "These elves have found—" He paused, and for a moment I thought I saw him shudder.

"What?" I cried. "What have they found?"

Fazwad looked grim. "Two of them were exploring the oldest part of the forest when they stumbled across an ancient temple. Inside was a statue. In the center of the statue was a great gem, which the fools pried loose and took back to their village. This gem is written of in the old books. It is called the 'Queen's Belly Button.' It has great powers. But it is also more dangerous than those elves could have guessed. It tempts and it lures and it draws you into evil. Those elves were once good. Now they are no longer to be trusted. I want you to get that stone and bring it back to me, Moongobble. *That* is your third Mighty Task."

"But how am I to keep from turning bad myself?" asked Moongobble.

"That's part of the task!" snapped Fazwad.

Moongobble frowned. "Aren't you afraid I might use my magic for evil?"

Fazwad threw back his head and laughed. "If you had any skill as a magician, I *might* worry about that. But that's one reason I chose you for this task. Even if you do go bad, it won't make any difference! What are you going to do? Turn everyone into cheese?"

He laughed nastily, then snapped his fingers and vanished in a cloud of blue smoke.

"I really don't like that guy," muttered Urk.

Turning around, I saw Arfur sitting on the table again.

"Where did you go?" I asked.

Arfur shrugged. "I was hanging from the edge of

the table. We don't like to be seen if we can help it."

"Did you hear all that?" asked Urk.

"Of course," said Arfur.

"Do you think it was true?" asked Moongobble.

"I *know* it's true! That's what I came to talk to you about. My cousins Urfur and Furbag were the ones who found the Queen's Belly Button. You remember them, Moongobble. They helped you too. Now they've gone bad. Really, really bad."

Moongobble had already made up his mind to accept the third Mighty Task, of course. But now that he knew that the elves who were in trouble were his friends, nothing could stop him.

"Let's get ready!" he cried. "The sooner we leave, the better!"

CHAPTER 4

READY FOR THE ADVENTURE

Getting ready for a quest didn't simply mean packing. First Moongobble had to decide what magical items to bring. This was a big job.

While Moongobble worked on his list, Urk and I went to ask the Rusty Knight if he would join us. After that, we had to do something I was not looking forward to: convince my parents to let *me* go. I wondered if it would be easier to convince Mother now that Father was back—or harder than ever. What if he was so glad we were all together again that *he* forbade me to go?

Putting Urk on my shoulder, I started down the

hill. "I'll tell you, Edward," he said after we had gone a little way, "I don't much like this."

"Why not?"

"If those elves are as dangerous as Fazwad says, he should send someone who can really handle them to do this. Unless . . ."

"Unless what?"

"Unless his plan is that they will do something terrible to Moongobble. Then, once Moongobble is out of the way, Fazwad can send in the whole Society of Magicians to deal with them."

I gasped. "Would he really plan something that nasty?"

Urk didn't answer. He didn't have to. I knew it was a stupid question. Of course Fazwad would do something that nasty!

Though my cottage is at the base of Moongobble's hill, we walked right past it. We would have better luck talking my parents into letting me go if the Rusty Knight was coming too, so I wanted to talk to him first.

The Rusty Knight is old, and his armor is creaky,

and he doesn't hear very well. But he was a great hero once, and he knows a lot about questing.

We found him outside his cottage, dressed in his armor and trimming some bushes with his sword. He creaked with every move he made.

"Hello, Edward!" he cried when he saw me. "Hello, Urk! What can I do for you?"

"Moongobble has his third Mighty Task," I said. "He has to deal with some evil elves."

"Evil smells?" asked the Rusty Knight. As I said, his hearing is not very good. "Well, I don't know much about battling smells, but I'll be glad to come along."

I thought about trying to explain, but decided not to. He would figure it out sooner or later. Maybe.

Our next stop was my cottage.

As I feared, Father said, "No, Edward. I don't want you to go. Now that our little family is together again, I want to keep it that way."

To my surprise, Mother disagreed. "If Edward had not gone with Moongobble the last time, we would not be together. I think he should go."

Father looked at her in surprise. I looked at her

in surprise. Urk looked at her in surprise. The Rusty Knight took off his helmet and started cleaning out his ears.

"Wait outside," said Father.

Urk, the Rusty Knight, and I stepped outside.

"Things will be fine," said Urk, after we closed the door.

"How do you know?" I asked.

The toad smiled. "Your mother has already made up your father's mind for him. He just doesn't know it yet."

"I don't know why they're so worried about evil smells anyway," muttered the Rusty Knight.

A few minutes later Mother and Father came out to join us. Father sighed, then said, "Your Mother and I think you should go, Edward."

Urk, who was sitting on my shoulder, made a tiny snort.

"Be good to those you meet along the way," said Mother, handing me a basket of food. Mother always gave us food to take along. I was glad of the food, but I didn't really need the advice that came with it. "Be good to those you meet along the way" is a basic rule for anyone going on a magical adventure.

We climbed back up the hill. Moongobble and Arfur were waiting for us.

"Ready to go?" asked Moongobble.

"Ready!" I said.

Moongobble nodded. "Good. Arfur has told me more about what is going on, and I am eager to help."

We packed our things in a magical wagon Moongobble had made. Well, it was really just a big wooden box. It had no wheels, and no place for a horse—or a human—to hold on to it.

"What good will that thing do?" asked the Rusty Knight.

"It will float behind us," said Moongobble. "Watch!"

He waved his wand at the wagon. It shot straight up into the air—then began to fall.

"Watch out!" cried Urk.

We all dived for cover.

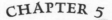

CHAPTER 5

STRANGE JOURNEY

I ended up under a bush. Peeking out, I saw the wagon stop about three inches above the ground. It made a big farting noise.

"Evil smells already!" cried the Rusty Knight, drawing his sword. He wasn't kidding. We all began to choke and gag. But the wagon seemed to have settled down.

Urk sighed. "Don't expect *me* to drive that thing. I'd rather hop!"

I put him on the ground.

Fireball fluttered down to take Urk's place on my shoulder.

Arfur climbed into his Winged Wonder and began to peddle.

With the wagon floating behind us, we headed into the forest behind Moongobble's cottage. I had never entered this forest before I met Moongobble. It is deep and dark, and the people of Pigbone tell strange tales about it. Now it did not frighten me. Moongobble and I often went there to gather things for his spells.

But this time we were going to go way past the forest. I knew there might be weird and frightening things between us and the elf village.

"How long will the journey take?" asked the Rusty Knight, who was clanking along at the rear.

"That depends," said Arfur.

"On what?" I asked.

Arfur shuddered. "On whether we walk *through* Bogfester Swamp, or make a big loop around it."

Urk croaked in alarm. "Bogfester Swamp? I vote we go around. Way, way around!"

"Why?" asked Moongobble.

"My mother used to tell me stories about that swamp," said Urk. "Strange things happen there."

I had never thought about Urk having a mother. I wondered what she was like. Of course, there were a lot of things I wondered about Urk, such as why he could talk. Whenever I asked him, he told me that there were things I was not yet ready to know.

This really annoyed me.

We made camp that night in a little grove beside a small waterfall. Going to sleep to the sound of the water was nice. It was like listening to music, which we don't get much of in Pigbone.

The next day we climbed up and up. The forest got thinner, and after a while we came to a rocky place where the trees were gone altogether. Soon we were walking along a cliff so high that looking down made me dizzy. Since Arfur and Fireball were flying, they did not have to stay on the path and would flap out over the deep drop as if it did not bother them at all.

I could hardly stand to watch.

It was harder to camp this night, but we finally found a cave where we thought we would be safe.

All through the night we heard strange cries in the distance.

"Mountain monsters," said Arfur, sleepily.

"Don't worry, they don't like people."

"That's what I'm worried about," I said.

Arfur laughed. "Oh, I meant they don't like people for supper!"

I worried anyway.

The next day we headed downhill. I was glad to see trees again, and even more glad when the steep drop was gone and I didn't have to be so careful where I walked.

Suddenly Arfur was fluttering near my head on the Winged Wonder. "Shhh!" he hissed. "Look over there!"

I glanced where he was pointing, then caught my breath. A unicorn stood beneath a nearby tree. It had a silky white mane and a gleaming horn that stuck straight out of its forehead. It was the most beautiful thing I had ever seen.

The unicorn watched us for a few minutes. Then it turned and trotted into the green darkness of the forest.

Not long after, we came to a deep crack in the Earth. It was about thirty feet across, and about a hundred feet to the bottom. What made it worse was that the bridge had fallen down.

"Drat!" said Arfur. "We'll have to go the other way after all."

"The other way?" I asked.

"Through Bogfester Swamp," he said, his voice fearful.

CHAPTER 6

BOGFESTER SWAMP

Bogfester Swamp was even worse than Urk had said. Its waters were brown and murky, and dotted with patches of green scum. A heavy mist hung over everything, making it hard to see. And a heavy stink made it even harder to breathe.

"Is this the evil smell we came to fight?" cried the Rusty Knight, pulling out his sword.

"Put that sword back!" bellowed Urk.

The Rusty Knight sighed and slid his sword into its sheath.

"How are we going to cross this mess?" I asked.

"There's supposed to be a path," said Arfur.

"Well, where is it?" asked Urk.

Arfur shrugged. "All I know is that the start of the path is marked by a pair of boulders that look like big fangs."

"I'll go look for them," said Fireball. Launching himself into the air, he flew off to the right.

An hour or so later he came flapping back. "Not that way," he said, and flew to the left.

Two minutes later he was back again. "They're right over there!" he said, sounding disgusted. "Follow me."

We tromped after him. Soon we saw two curving stones, each about ten feet high. Fireball flapped his way between them.

The path was narrow. The muck on either side bubbled and popped. Mist floated around our knees, making it hard to see where we put our feet. The soggy ground squished beneath our shoes. A few times I missed the path and slipped into water, sometimes up to my ankle, sometimes all the way to my knee.

After an hour or so of this, Fireball—who has the best hearing of any of us—hissed, "What's that?"

"What's what?" I asked.

"I don't hear anything," said the Rusty Knight, which was almost certainly true.

"That!" said Fireball.

This time I heard it, too—an old lady's voice, crying, "Help! Help! Save me!"

"Drat," said Urk. "We'd better go see if we can help."

Arfur looked alarmed. "If you step into the swamp, you could be lost forever," he warned.

"Worse things than that can happen if you ignore an old lady who needs help," replied Urk. "Especially in a place like this."

"Let's all get on the wagon," said Moongobble. "Fireball, if I throw you a rope, can you pull us toward the screams?"

"I can try," said the little dragon, sounding doubtful.

We climbed onto the floating wagon. To my surprise, it didn't sink any closer to the ground than it was already. Then we discovered a new problem: we didn't have a rope.

Moongobble groaned. "Now what?"

"The belt from your robe," I said. "Use that!"

"Excellent idea!" cried Moongobble.

Taking the belt from around his waist, he tossed one end to Fireball, who was hovering just above us. Moongobble held the other end himself. Fireball lunged forward and we began to skim over the murky water. Foul mists swirled around us, so thick it was as if we were riding through clouds. But the trunks of the dead trees made it clear we were not in the sky.

Soon we saw an old lady standing on a small rise of ground. Long brown tentacles rose from the water around her, trying to grab her. She was beating at them with a stick. Whenever she hit a tentacle, it would slither into the water. At once another would rise from the other side of her.

"Climb onto the wagon!" shouted Moongobble as Fireball pulled us closer to her.

The old woman reached for the wagon. As she did, a tentacle wrapped around her ankle. She whacked it with her stick. The tentacle let go. The Rusty Knight and I grabbed the old woman's arms and pulled her aboard.

"Thank you!" she gasped. *"Thank you!"*

A tentacle grabbed the edge of the wagon, tipping us sideways.

"It's got us!" shouted Fireball, flapping harder.

The Rusty Knight smacked the tentacle with his sword. It let go and the wagon shot forward, nearly bumping Fireball in the rear. He began to fly even faster. Before long we reached the far side of Bogfester Swamp. We all started to cheer—except Fireball, who fluttered back and collapsed next to me. "I'm pooped!" he panted.

"You did great!" I whispered, patting his scaly head.

Then all of us—except Fireball—climbed off the wagon.

"Thank you," said the old woman, once we were on dry land. "I would have been swamp food if you had not come along."

"What were you doing in Bogfester anyway?" croaked Urk.

"Fleeing a great evil. My cottage is near an elf village. The elves used to be sweet. Now they have gone bad. *Very* bad."

"That's probably why they smell," said the Rusty Knight.

"Have no fear, madam," said Moongobble. "We have come to end this evil!"

The woman's eyes grew wide. "Better to stay away!" she warned.

"We cannot," replied Moongobble firmly.

The old woman reached into her pocket and pulled out a black bag. "Then take this," she said. "It may save your lives."

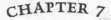

CHAPTER 7

WHO WILL GO?

We all looked at the cloth.

Finally I said, "What good will *that* do?"

"Do you know why the elves have gone bad?" replied the old woman.

"Because of the stone called the Queen's Belly Button," said Moongobble.

She nodded. "And the only way to help them is to get that stone away from them. But if you try, what is to stop you from turning evil yourselves?"

"We're still working on that," said Moongobble, sounding a little embarrassed.

"So brave," sighed the old lady. "And so foolish! All right, listen. There are two ways to block the stone's spell."

"What are they?" I asked eagerly.

"The first and hardest way is with the power of a good heart."

"My cousins have good hearts!" protested Arfur. "It didn't save them."

"They did not have advance warning," said the old woman. "You do. You know what the stone is and what it can do. Whoever carries it must fight with all his might to hold on to what he knows is good."

"How do you do that?" I asked.

"Think of the good things in your life. Think of the people who love you. Hold them in your heart. They will be your shield against evil. Still, it's tricky, and will take constant struggle. So here is the easier way. Put the Queen's Belly Button inside this bag. It will block the spell."

"She could have just told us that to begin with," muttered Urk.

"My thanks, madam!" said Moongobble.

Before he could say anything else, we heard a

sound. Turning, we saw four elves running toward us. I got ready to fight, though it didn't seem as if it could be much of a battle when they were so small.

But they didn't want to fight. "Arfur!" they called. "Arfur! Thank goodness we've found you!"

"Bilbog!" cried Arfur. "Dimstat! Thignum! Borfle! What are you doing here? I thought you were out on a quest."

"We were," said the first of them. "We just got back last night. Oh, Arfur, it was awful! It's as if everyone has gone crazy. What has happened to our home?"

"Come over here, and we'll explain," said Moongobble.

As the four elves started toward us, I turned to say something to the old lady. To my surprise, she was gone.

We looked, but could find no sign of her.

"Just what you'd expect from an old woman you met in Bogfester Swamp," muttered Urk.

Arfur had been talking to the other elves while the rest of us looked for the old lady. "Listen," he said. "Things are worse than we thought. Bilbog told me that the elves are making plans to take over the whole kingdom! We have to do something—fast! They could start a war between the magicians and the elves that would mean doom and destruction for everyone!"

"We can't do anything until we know more," said Urk. "One of us should do some spying."

"The only ones who can spy in an elf village are elves," pointed out Moongobble.

"That's no good," said Arfur. "We're all too well known."

"Then we must shrink one of us," said Moongobble.

"Stink one of us?" said the Rusty Knight. "Is that how we're going to fight the evil smell?"

"*Shrink!*" bellowed Urk. "We're going to *shrink* one of us."

"Who are we going to shrink?" asked the Rusty Knight.

"Me, of course," said Moongobble. "This is my Mighty Task."

Arfur laughed. "No one is going to believe you're an elf, Moongobble! You look too old. That goes for you, too," he said, before the Rusty Knight could volunteer.

Suddenly I knew who it had to be. "I'll do it," I said. "Remember, I'm very good at sneaking."

"We can't send you, Edward," said Moongobble. "We're supposed to keep you *out* of real danger."

"I think we *have* to send Edward," said Urk. "This quest has changed. It isn't just to let you keep doing magic now. It's to save the kingdom from a terrible war!"

"Urk is right," said Arfur. "Edward is our only chance."

Suddenly I wondered if this was such a good idea after all.

While Arfur taught me how to pretend to be an elf, the others went looking for the things Moongobble needed to make a shrinking potion. All too soon they were back and it was time for me to get small.

I wondered if Moongobble would really shrink me—or just turn me into cheese.

CHAPTER 8

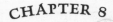

SHRINKING

"I don't do potions very well," said Moongobble, sounding worried.

He was stirring a pot. In the pot were the things my friends had gathered, including tiny mushrooms, an earthworm's eyebrow, several ant toes, and some fuzz from a baby bird.

"Fuzz from a baby bird?" I had cried.

"Don't worry," said Urk. "The little tweeter is fine. His mother gave it to me."

Moongobble tossed other things in the kettle, too, including some stuff he had brought from the cottage.

It was the worst smelling brew I'd ever sniffed, like a combination of dead fish and rotten cabbage.

The Rusty Knight looked puzzled. "I thought we came to *fight* an evil smell, not make one," he muttered.

The potion bubbled and boiled for hours, getting thicker and smellier as it did. Finally the kettle held only a cup of brew.

Moongobble scooped it out and handed it to me. It was thick and nasty looking.

"Do I have to *drink* this?" I asked.

"Not if you don't want to," he said gently. "But it's the only way to shrink you."

Holding my nose, I tipped the cup into my mouth.

"*Bluch!*" I cried. "That's awful!"

Then my head began to spin.

When I opened my eyes, I didn't feel any different. I thought the potion hadn't worked, until I glanced around. Next to me was an oak leaf that looked as big as my bed. Beside the leaf was an acorn I would have needed both hands to lift.

"How do you feel, Edward?"

I looked up and screamed. Moongobble towered above me, bigger than any giant I could have imagined. Fireball was next to him, to my eyes no longer a little dragon, but a huge monster.

I felt a hand on my shoulder and spun around. It was Arfur, who was now exactly the same height as me. Next to him squatted Urk. His wide mouth was bigger than my head. If he had been willing, I could have ridden him like a pony.

"How can you stand it?" I asked Arfur.

The elf looked puzzled. "What do you mean?"

"Isn't the world too scary for you?"

Arfur smiled. "If you've been this size all your life, it just seems normal. You'll get used to it."

I looked up again. The Rusty Knight was bending toward me. His mustache looked like a gray hedgerow.

"I don't think I'll ever get used to *this*!" I said.

"Things won't be so bad once you're in the village," said Arfur. "Everyone there will be the same size as you. They'll all be evil, of course, because of the stone. But at least they'll be the same size as you. Let's switch clothes."

I didn't want to undress in front of everyone, so Arfur and I went behind a tree.

"Very good!" said Urk when we came out. "There's only one problem."

"What?" I asked.

"Your ears. They're too round for you to be an elf."

I touched my ears. Urk was right.

Moongobble waved his wand over me and said, "Iggle Biggle Eerzum Grope Oints!"

I saw a flash of blue light. It felt as if someone was pulling on my ears.

"Good grief!" cried Urk. "That actually worked. You may finally be getting the hang of this, Moongobble!"

I touched the tips of my ears. They were indeed pointed like an elf's. "I guess I'd better be on my way," I said, a little nervously.

"Not yet," said Arfur. "First you have to learn to fly."

"Won't the elves be more likely to notice me that way?"

"Not if you fly in at night and hide the Winged Wonder before you enter the village. I know a place where you can do that. If you get in trouble, it will be harder for them to catch you if you can fly."

I hadn't thought about the evil elves trying to catch me. It was scary.

Arfur gave me some tips on how to ride the Winged Wonder, then said, "All right, give it a try!"

I hopped on and began to pedal. The wings flapped, but I didn't move.

"Pedal harder!" shouted Arfur. "Pedal harder!"

I pedaled harder.

Suddenly the Winged Wonder lifted into the air.

"Look!" I shouted. "I'm flying!"

Arfur cried, "Edward, watch out!"

CHAPTER 9

SPYING

Arfur's warning came just in time. I was heading for a tree. Wrenching the handlebars to the side, I barely missed the trunk. Spotting a branch above me I dipped down—and almost ran into a branch beneath me.

How in the world do birds do this without killing themselves? I wondered as I plunged through a mass of leaves.

"Pull up, Edward!" shouted the elves.

"And pedal harder!" added Arfur.

The ground was rushing toward me. I pumped

the pedals with all my might. Just in time I pulled out of my dive. Swooping above the elves' heads, I shot back into the air. This was harder than I thought!

When I finally felt I knew how to steer the thing, I landed next to my friends.

"Very exciting," muttered Urk. "Remind me to wear a blindfold the next time you try something like that."

At twilight everyone wished me luck and told me to be careful.

That's when we discovered the new problem. The bag the old woman had given us was too big for me to carry!

"Now what do we do?" muttered Fireball.

Moongobble looked at me seriously. "Edward, I have always believed you to have a good heart. Do you think you can fight the evil of this stone?"

I swallowed hard. "I can try."

"Then bring it back as quickly as you can. We'll be waiting with the bag."

Feeling more frightened than ever, I climbed

onto the Winged Wonder and headed for the village. After about twenty minutes of flying, I came to the clearing where Arfur had said I would find it.

As I glided out from the trees, I saw the sky above me, dark and clear and filled with twinkling stars. For a moment I wanted to fly up and up, just to see if I could reach them.

Settle down! I told myself. *You've got a job to do!*

In the center of the clearing stood a giant oak tree.

In the branches of the oak tree was the elf village.

I landed on a thick branch, fairly far down the tree. As Arfur had promised, when I rolled the Winged Wonder up to the trunk, I found a hole just big enough for me to hide the machine in.

Well, a hole in a tree wasn't such an odd thing. But a tiny stairway carved into the side of the tree certainly was.

I started to climb. The stairs wound around and around, up the inside of the tree. After a hundred steps, I came to a door, just as Arfur had said I would. I opened it, and stepped out into the most amazing place I had ever seen.

Pigbone only has fifteen buildings. The elf village had hundreds! I had never imagined anyplace could be that big. Well, not *big* big; everything was pretty small, of course. But all along the branches of the great oak were elven houses, and elven shops, and elven taverns . . . and elves! Hundreds of them hurrying from place to place.

I noticed they were all frowning and glaring at each other. This wasn't the way I thought elves would be. Then I realized it must be the stone that made them act this way. Even so, I didn't understand how bad things really were until I passed a side branch and heard someone crying.

Looking to my right, I saw a squirrel tied to a branch.

"What happened to *you*?" I asked.

I didn't really expect an answer. Only a few of the animals I've met can talk. It turned out this squirrel was one of them. She sniffed a few times, then said, "Three elves grabbed me and tied me down. They laughed while they did it, and told me I didn't belong here! How can a squirrel not belong in a tree?"

I took out my knife to cut her loose.

"All right, all right, I don't belong in a tree!" cried the squirrel.

She thought I was one of the evil elves!

"Shhh!" I whispered. "I'm not going to hurt you. I'm going to *free* you!"

Glancing around to make sure no evil elves could see me, I cut the ropes.

"Thank you!" whispered the squirrel. Then she scampered off.

I continued up the tree. Most of the elves ignored me. Some of them snarled at me. One offered to fight me, but I hurried past and he picked a fight with someone else instead.

The higher I climbed, the worse things got. It was as if the closer the elves were to the stone, the more they were affected. I heard elves say things that would have gotten my mouth washed out with soap. I saw elves building booby traps for their neighbors. And I felt greater danger with every level I climbed.

Finally I reached the main level of the elf village. The buildings here were bigger, and many had signs on them. ACORN LODGE, A RESTING PLACE FOR WEARY TRAVELERS said one. At least, it had said that, before someone painted GO AWAY! over those words in big black letters. HONEY AND NUTS said another. It looked as if it had been a nice place. Now its windows were broken and its door was boarded over.

I walked until I found a building labeled TOWN HALL. Next to it was the building I was looking for: MUSEUM said a big sign on the front.

I went in.

Dozens of elves were crowded inside, all staring at a pedestal.

Resting on the pedestal was a glittering stone.

I felt a sudden urge to kick the elf standing next to me.

No doubt about it. I had found the Queen's Belly Button.

CHAPTER 10

THE POWER OF THE STONE

I slipped out of the museum and moved quickly away from it. After a few minutes I found an unused branch. I climbed as far along it as I dared, until I was sitting on little more than twigs. I was so light the twigs barely bent beneath me. But every time the wind blew, they shifted in a scary way.

I couldn't see the ground—other branches blocked the view.

I closed my eyes and thought about my home, and my parents. I thought of all the good things I could, to fight off the evil of the stone.

I sat that way as darkness fell. For a long time the elf village stayed awake. I heard shouting and fighting, and several very naughty songs that sounded like they were being sung by elves who had drunk too much acorn wine.

At last all fell silent. I climbed back toward the village. Most of the elves had gone into their houses, but I had to pick my way around others who lay in the middle of the wooden paths, snoring little elf snores. I hoped none of them would roll over in their sleep. They might fall off, and it was a long way down.

The guards at the museum door were asleep too.

I stepped over them and went to the center of the museum. Three dimly glowing torches surrounded the stone. I picked it up and tucked it into my shirt.

At once there was a horrible shrieking. They must have put an alarm spell on the stone!

As I raced out of the museum, the guards stumbled to their feet crying, "Stop! Stop, you thief!"

Other elves woke and started to chase me. They were sleepy, which slowed them down. But trying to find my way along the twisting branches with only moonlight to guide me slowed me down too.

Just when the elves were about to catch me, a voice cried, "This way!"

I looked to my right. It was the squirrel I had cut free.

"Climb on my back!" she cried.

I scrambled on. The angry, shouting elves were right behind us.

The squirrel leaped into the air. I think I screamed. We hurtled down about ten feet—which at my size seemed more like a hundred feet—when

suddenly she grabbed a branch. It swung and swayed, flipping us back and forth. I clung to the squirrel's fur as if my life depended on it.

The squirrel carried me to where I had hidden the Winged Wonder. I thanked her and hugged her good-bye. Then I climbed into Arfur's flying machine.

As I pedaled, I could feel the Queen's Belly Button burning against my own belly button. *Don't give in,* I told myself. *Don't give in!*

Still fighting the power of the stone, I fluttered down into our camp.

Moongobble and the others rushed to greet me.

Reaching into my shirt, I pulled out the Queen's Belly Button. I meant to hand it to Moongobble. I *wanted* to hand it to Moongobble. But to my own astonishment I heard myself shout: "Get back, all of you. Get back or . . . or . . . or I'll turn you into cheese!"

CHAPTER 11

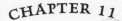

ME, MYSELF, AND I

My friends dropped back, their faces filled with shock, surprise, and horror.

"Wait!" I said. "I didn't really mean it."

Moongobble and the others stopped. But they didn't move toward me. They just stood where they were, looking puzzled, and a little afraid.

Suddenly I was glad that they looked afraid! At least, part of me was glad. Another part of me didn't like it at all.

I felt as if I had been cut into pieces. Part of me wanted to do bad things. Part of me was horrified by

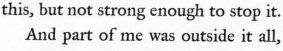

this, but not strong enough to stop it. And part of me was outside it all, thinking how strange it was.

"Are you all right, Edward?" asked the Rusty Knight.

I turned around and stuck my butt out. Then I wiggled it at him.

"This doesn't look good," muttered Urk.

"Quiet, toad!" I shouted. "Or I'll turn you into a polliwog. Or maybe an egg. Then I'll feed you to a fish."

The part of me watching all this was getting even more unhappy. The Rusty Knight and Urk were my friends. It wasn't right to be rude to them.

Shut up, you little goody-goody! thought the part of me that was feeling evil.

How strange! thought the part of me that was watching it all.

Moongobble stepped toward me. He put out his hand and said gently, "Edward, I think you should give me the stone."

"Stand back, old man!" I shouted.

Fireball hissed angrily.

I turned the stone toward him. I swear I did not say or do anything. Even so, a bolt of power shot out of it.

Moongobble raised his wand and cried, "Argle Bargle Dezap Dezotz!"

I heard a sizzling sound. Something shot out of Moongobble's wand. It caught my bolt of power. With a flare of light, both pieces of magic were gone.

I was amazed that Moongobble could do that.

Which made me think of how hard we had been working for him to become a magician.

The nice part of me remembered what the old woman in the swamp had said about holding on to the good things in my life, holding onto thoughts of the people who loved me.

I started trying to do that, trying to think only of those things. I thought about my mother. I remembered the smell of her bread, and the way she kissed me good night.

Don't be stupid! snarled the bad part of me.

I thought about working for Moongobble.

He doesn't pay you enough! snapped my evil self. *You should zap him!*

I thought about having a dragon and a toad and a knight for friends.

Don't you know any normal people? scoffed my bad side.

I thought about finding my father and bringing him home.

My bad side said nothing.

Interesting, thought the part that was just watching things. *That seems to have shut up your bad side.*

Maybe you should hold on to that thought.

I held on to the thought, and the memories of all the other good things in my life.

I could feel myself getting dizzy, but I kept holding on, until I heard Urk shout, "Watch out, he's going down!"

Everything went black, and I fell face first to the ground.

CHAPTER 12

FAZWAD AT HIS WORST

When I opened my eyes again, the forest seemed to be drifting by overhead. It took me a moment to realize that I was in the floating cart.

"Welcome back, Edward!" said a voice.

Turning my head, I saw Urk. He seemed to be normal sized—which meant I must have grown back to my own normal size while I was asleep.

"Are you all right?" called Fireball. He was flying just above me.

"I don't know." I rubbed my head. "What happened?"

"You were completely worn out from fighting the evil of the stone," said Urk. "We put you in the wagon so we could start for home. We're almost there."

Suddenly I remembered what I had done. "I am so sorry!" I cried. "I can't believe how I acted!"

"Oh, stop," said Urk. "The problem was the stone, not you."

"And you beat the stone's power," said the Rusty Knight. "You must have a noble heart. Only someone with a noble heart could have fought the stone that way."

"I can't wait to see old Fazwad's face when he finds out we actually managed to do this," called Arfur. He was sitting at the end of the wagon, with his feet dangling inside. "He's going to be furious!"

"I need to think about what to do when I see him," said Moongobble. I realized he was walking beside us.

"What's to think about?" asked Urk. "If Fazwad gets too rotten, just turn the stone against him. It will pull out all his power!"

I loved this idea. I knew that the stone really

could take Fazwad's power. But Moongobble looked disturbed.

By the time we arrived at the cottage, I was feeling good enough to help with the unpacking. We were just sitting down to discuss how we should handle Fazwad when we heard a snap and saw a puff of blue smoke.

It was Fazwad, of course. Showing up that soon after we got back ourselves made me wonder if he had been spying on the cottage. He looked at us sitting around the table and curled his lip. Then he turned to Moongobble and said, "Well, how did you do?"

"I've got the stone right here," said Moongobble. Reaching into his pocket, he pulled out the black bag.

Fazwad looked startled. "You do not!"

Moongobble smiled and turned the bag over, dumping the stone into his hand. I was surprised to see how small it was. I was also surprised to see that it didn't seem to bother him at all to hold it.

Fazwad's eyes widened. Then he began to laugh. "Do you really think that's going to do you any good?

We cannot let you into the society, you boob. You never would have done it if you hadn't had help."

"That's not fair!" I cried, jumping to my feet.

"Fairness has nothing to do with it," said Fazwad, sounding as if I were some sort of fool. "What matters is that he could not have done it on his own."

"You never said he couldn't have help!" bellowed Urk.

I felt a rush of fury. But before I could speak, Moongobble dropped the stone back into the bag. I had never seen him look so angry. "Here," he said, holding the bag out to Fazwad. "Take it. Take it, and leave this house."

I couldn't believe my ears.

"No!" I cried. "You can't let him have it!"

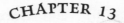

CHAPTER 13

THE FINAL TEST

For a moment, no one moved. Fazwad stared at Moongobble, his eyes dark and hard. It was as if he was trying to see right through him.

Then, to my surprise, he took the bag and said, "Well done, Moongobble. We will see that the stone is returned to its rightful place."

Then something even more amazing happened.

Fazwad smiled. Not his usual nasty, sneering smile. This was actually a nice smile. I had seen a lot of strange things since I started working for Moongobble, but I think that smile was the strangest thing of all.

"I don't understand," said Moongobble.

Fazwad's smile grew broader. If I didn't know better, I would have thought he actually looked . . . nice! Tucking his hands behind him, he said, "I'm pleased to say that you have just succeeded at your Third Mighty Task."

He actually sounded happy.

"You are being very confusing," said Urk.

"I suppose I am," said Fazwad. "All right, it's time for the truth. We all know that Moongobble has a lot of trouble with his magic."

He paused, as if waiting for us to admit that this was the truth. I wanted to deny it, but that was silly. Too many things—including me—had been turned into cheese to say that was not true.

"Yet Moongobble does have promise," said Fazwad. "So it was important for me to make sure he could really do the job. Magic is not easy. It takes skill and training and hard work. But more than all that, it takes good heart—good heart even when people are not being good to you. That is why I have been so nasty to you, Moongobble. I had to test not only your ability to accomplish these Mighty Tasks, but also how you would react to someone who was being mean to you. Your third Mighty Task was not really to get the Queen's Belly Button, though that was very important and it is a great relief to have it safe. The real test came just now, when you could have used it against me, but chose not to."

He reached out his hand. "Moongobble, you are now a member of the Society of Magicians."

The mice in Moongobble's hat began to cheer.

"You will have more quests, and many more difficult tasks," continued Fazwad. "But you will also have the help and friendship of your brother magicians. I welcome you to the society."

That night we had a big party in front of Moongobble's cottage. We built a bonfire and ate wonderful food that Mother had cooked.

The Rusty Knight was there, of course. So were Urk and Fireball. Arfur stayed with us, too. But the biggest surprise of all was that Fazwad came and brought ten magicians with him.

"We have word from the elf village that your relatives have completely recovered," Fazwad told Arfur, which made the little elf dance with happiness.

The magicians had brought more food (though none of it was as good as Mother's). They taught Moongobble the secret handshake of the Society of Magicians. They told songs and jokes and stories. And just before midnight they put on a huge fireworks display. As fountains of light filled the sky, I

could hear the people down in Pigbone crying out in wonder.

The last firework of all exploded in huge red letters that wrote across the sky, "MOONGOBBLE IS A MAGICIAN!"

It was the best night of my life.

ABOUT THE AUTHOR AND ILLUSTRATOR

BRUCE COVILLE is the author of nearly ninety books for young readers, including the international best-seller *My Teacher Is an Alien*. He has been a teacher, a toymaker, a cookware salesman, and a grave digger. In addition to his work as an author, Bruce is much in demand as a speaker and as a storyteller. He is also the founder and president of Full Cast Audio, a company dedicated to producing unabridged recordings of children's books in a full-cast format. For more information about Bruce check out www.brucecoville.com.

KATHERINE COVILLE is an artist, sculptor, and doll maker who specializes in highly detailed images of creatures never before seen in this world. She has illustrated several books written by her husband, Bruce Coville, including *Goblins in the Castle, Aliens Ate My Homework,* and the Space Brat series.

Bruce and Katherine live in Syracuse, New York, with a varying assortment of pets and children.